Oh No, GEORGE!

Freedom is secured not by the fulfilling of one's desires, but by the removal of desire... No man is free who is not master of himself.

Epictetus

For Loonie xx

First published 2012 by Walker Books Ltd
87 Vauxhall Walk, London SE11 5HJ

10 9 8 7 6 5 4 3 2 1

This book has been typeset in A Bit Lost Regular

Printed in Belgium

British Library Cataloguing in Publication Data: a catalogue record for this book is available from the British Library.

ISBN 978-1-4603-3225-4

www.walker.co.uk

WALKER BOOKS
AND SUBSIDIARIES
LONDON · BOSTON · SYDNEY · AUCKLAND

Oh No, GEORGE!

CHRIS HAUGHTON

Harris is going out.
"Will you be good, George?"
asks Harris.

"Yes," says George.
"I'll be very good."

I hope I'll be good,
George thinks.

George sees
something
in the kitchen.

It's cake!
I said I'd be good,
George thinks,
but I LOVE cake.

What will George do?

Oh no, George!

What has George
seen now?

It's Cat!
I said I'd be good,
George thinks,
but I LOVE to play
with Cat.

What will George do?

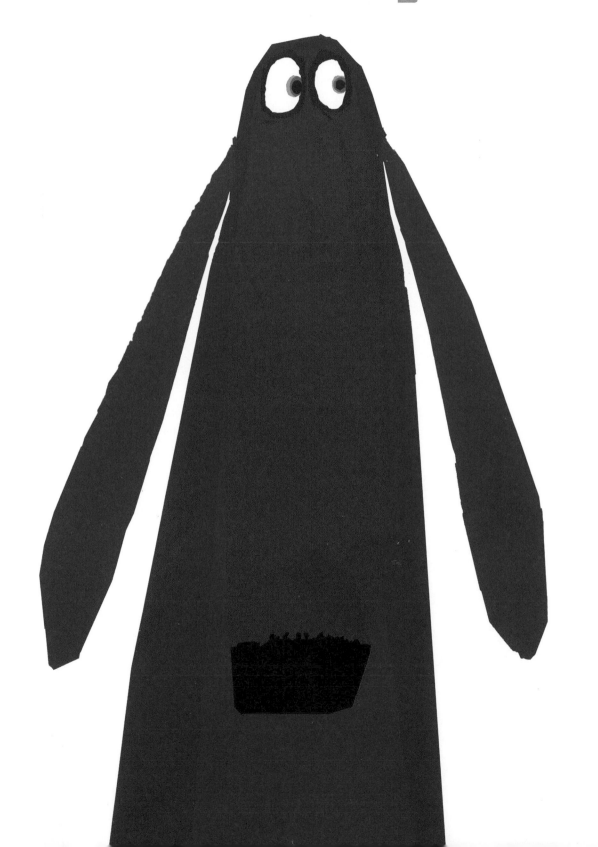

Oh no, George!

What has George
seen now?

Some lovely soil!
I said I'd be good,
George thinks,
but I LOVE
to dig soil.

What will George do?

Oh no, George!

Harris is back.
"Hello, Harris!
Great to see you!"

"George! What have you done?
You've RUINED the place...

"And how on earth did you
eat a WHOLE cake?"

I said I'd be good,
George thinks,
I hoped I'd be good,
but I wasn't.

What will George do?

"I'm sorry," George says.
"I want to give you
my favourite toy."

"Thank you, George," says Harris.
"Why don't we go out
for a nice walk?"

Great! George loves to go out. There are so many things to see and do.

Uh-oh. George has seen a cake. Will he eat it?

No. George goes
straight past.
Well done, George!

George sees
some lovely soil.
Will he have a
little dig?

No.
Well done,
George!

George doesn't even try to chase Cat. Even Cat is a bit surprised.

Something smells
very interesting.
What can it be?

It's a rubbish bin. There's nothing
George likes more than rubbish.

What will George do?

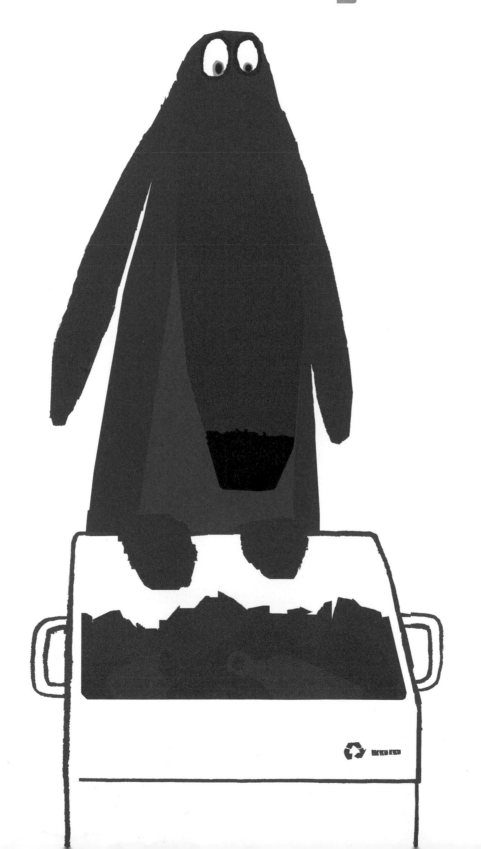

George?

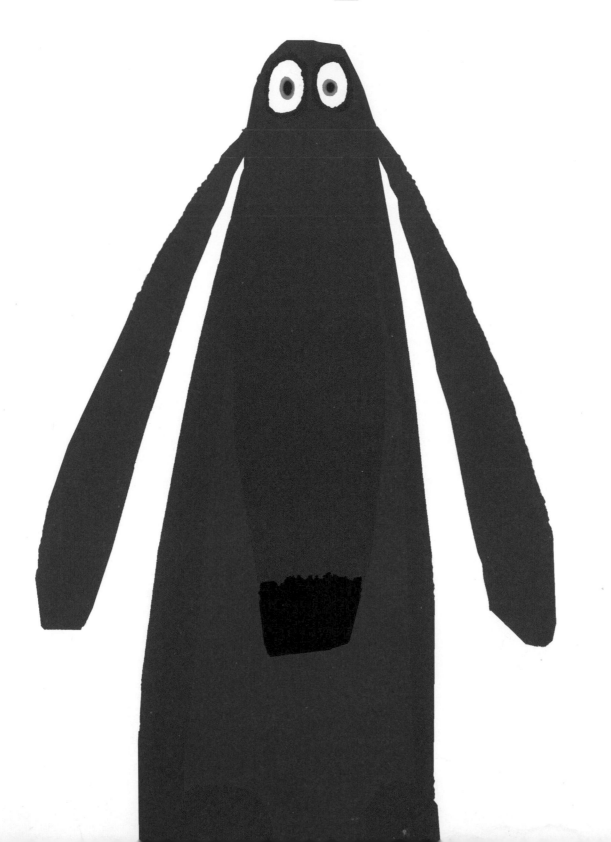